Taking Care of Sister Bear

Taking Care of
Sister Bear

Ursel Scheffler
illustrated by Ulises Wensell

A DOUBLEDAY BOOK FOR YOUNG READERS

"Hold me, too, Mama!" cried Little Bear.

"But you're too heavy," said Mama Bear, and she rocked little Sister Bear back and forth.

"I'm not heavy at all," said Little Bear. "Look!" And he jumped onto the chair and the table and back down again. "I'm as light as a feather."

"Little Bear, you're not a baby anymore!"

"But I'm not a big bear yet, not as big as Papa."

"You're big enough to play outside while I feed your baby sister," said Mama Bear.

So Little Bear went outside.

Little Bear frowned at the branches and pieces of bark that had once been a wonderful tower. Sister Bear had knocked it all down with her clumsy paws. Having a little sister was no fun at all! She ruined everything, and everything revolved around her. If only his friend Willy would come to play! Little Bear hadn't seen him for days. He grumpily began rebuilding his tower.

"What a beautiful tower, Little Bear!" rumbled Papa Bear. He was bringing honey back from the forest.

"It was much prettier before," growled Little Bear.

They ate the honeycombs for lunch. Little Bear's sister didn't get any.

"She's still too young for that," said Mama Bear. "She would get sticky honey all over her."

Little Bear was glad he was bigger, because honey was his very favorite food.

After lunch, Papa and Mama Bear went off to pick berries and mushrooms.

"Take care of Sister Bear," said Mama Bear. "You can play with her outside when she wakes up from her nap."

"But don't go too far away," said Papa Bear. "We'll be back before it gets dark."

Just as Papa and Mama Bear disappeared into the forest, there was a knock at the door. Little Bear ran to the window. It was his friend Willy at last!

"Are you coming to the river? I have a new fishing rod. We can try it out," called Willy.

"I can't," said Little Bear sadly. "I have to watch my baby sister. She's still sleeping."

"Wake her up. We'll take her with us," said Willy.

The three bears went off down the path. It took forever to get to the river. Sister Bear was always stopping to pick flowers, nibble on berries or catch butterflies.

When they got to the water, Sister Bear sat down to watch a raccoon do her washing. Sister Bear liked the shiny soap bubbles that floated in the air. They were much more fun than the silly walk, which had made her paws sore.

"Come on!" Little Bear shouted. He grabbed her arm
and pulled.

Sister Bear cried. She didn't want to take another step.

"Little sisters can really be a pain!" groaned Little Bear.

"Give her to me," said Willy. "I've always wanted
a sister."

"She's yours," said Little Bear, "for a basketful of fish."

"Come," said Willy gently, and he took Sister Bear's
paw. At last they reached the bridge over the river, the
best fishing spot around.

They didn't catch any fish with the new fishing rod, because Sister Bear kept splashing in the water.

"You should take better care of her," said Little Bear. "After all, she'll soon be yours."

When Sister Bear got tired, she fell asleep on the grass. At last it was peaceful. Now they caught fish! Willy laughed and said, "Just wait. The basket will be full soon. Then I'll have a sister!"

But when the basket was full, Sister Bear was gone!
Where was she hiding? Little Bear and Willy looked
everywhere, calling and calling.

They searched in the forest until it got dark.

"I think I have to go home now," said Willy quietly. He was afraid of the dark.

"I'll keep looking," said Little Bear bravely. "I have to find her." Maybe he had given her away, but she was still his baby sister.

Little Bear ran back through the forest. Where could she be? Where? His heart pounded. Suddenly he smelled a bear. Was that his sister? He followed the pawprints. In the moonlight he saw the shadows of two bears. And he heard voices calling, "Little Bear! Little Bear!"

"Papa! Mama!" called Little Bear. He ran into their arms. And there was Sister Bear!

She had walked back along the river, and the raccoon had brought her home. Little Bear was so happy! Mama and Papa Bear were so glad to have Little Bear back safely that they forgot to be mad at him. Papa took Little Bear in his arms, and Mama held Sister Bear. "We looked everywhere for you," said Papa Bear. "You can't imagine how worried we were."

"Oh, yes I can," said Little Bear. "It feels terrible when someone you love is missing." And then he gave his baby sister a big fat bear kiss.

A DOUBLEDAY BOOK FOR YOUNG READERS

Published by

Bantam Doubleday Dell Publishing Group, Inc.

1540 Broadway, New York, New York 10036

First American Edition 1999
Originally published in Germany by Ravensburger Buchverlag
Doubleday and the portrayal of an anchor with a dolphin are trademarks of
Bantam Doubleday Dell Publishing Group, Inc.
Title of the original German edition: Kein Kuss für Bärenschwester
© 1998 Ravensburger Buchverlag GmbH (Germany)

Library of Congress Cataloging-in-Publication Data
ISBN: 0-385-32660-2
Cataloging-in-Publication Data is available from the U.S. Library of Congress.

The text of this book is set in 16.5-point Goudy. • Book design by Semadar Megged
Manufactured in Germany • September 1999
10 9 8 7 6 5 4 3 2 1